Dragon Booster™

THE CHOOSING

DRAGON BOOSTER

THE CHOOSING

Adapted by James Gelsey
Based on an original script
written by Rob Travalino
Created by
Kevin Mowrer
Rob Travalino

an imprint of
HYPERION BOOKS FOR CHILDREN
New York

TM The Story Hat Properties, LLC, used under license by Alliance Atlantis.
© 2004 ApolloScreen GmbH and Co. Filmproduktion KG. © 2003 The Story Hat Properties, LLC. All Rights Reserved.
Alliance Atlantis with the stylized "A" design is a trademark of Alliance Atlantis Communications Inc.
The Story Hat Logo is a trademark of The Story Hat, LLC.

Volo® is a registered trademark of Disney Enterprises, Inc.
Volo/Hyperion Books for Children are imprints of
Disney Children's Book Group, L.L.C.

Printed in the United States of America

First Edition
1 3 5 7 9 10 8 6 4 2

This book is set in 13.5 New Aster.

ISBN 0-7868-3771-3

CHAPTER 1

A new day had just begun in Sun City, and traffic was already snarled on Dragway 1138.

Sun City was the seventh and uppermost level of Dragon City. The rest of Dragon City extended nineteen miles directly below. Sun City's altitude meant it was the only part of Dragon City ever to receive direct sunlight. It also meant that Sun City sometimes felt like an oven.

Despite the heat, thousands of people

were jammed dragon to dragon on their way to work. Sun City was home to Dragon City's government and most of its big business. The place also attracted Dragon City's most powerful citizens. Among them was Word Paynn, the wealthiest man in all of Dragon City.

Word Paynn gazed out from his balcony at the top of the Paynn Incorporated tower. The tower was one of the highest points in Sun City. It gave Word a perfect view of all of Sun City's shimmering steel-and-glass structures.

Those ultramodern buildings represented Dragon City's most recent building boom over the past two hundred years.

Surveying the scene before him, Word's eyes fell upon the Elite Class racing track immediately below his tower. The track weaved through Dragon City. It offered Elite Class dragon racers the chance to show off their skills in the most highly competitive racing circuit around. In a short while, the track would explode with excitement as the first of many dragon races got under way.

The vast majority of the valued dragon gear used by racers to control and to enhance their dragons was manufactured by Paynn's company. The demand for this gear was not limited to Elite Class racers.

Anyone with dreams of riding a dragon owned at least one piece of gear. The Elite Class gear was a hundred times more powerful than the street gear used by some racers. The more powerful gear helped make Word Paynn a very wealthy man. But at this particular moment, he wasn't thinking about dragon races.

He stepped back into his command center. Word's attention immediately shifted to the enormous plasma screens lining the walls. Images of dragons—some in full racing gear and others clashing in epic battles—filled the screens. Staring at the large monitors, Word took a deep breath.

"The dragon is power," Word began. "Once, they were our equals. Today, humans control the dragon: to race, compete, and fight, at speeds nearing two hundred miles an hour."

Word paused. He heard a sound from the other side of the room. Someone had shifted his weight from one foot to the other and then crossed his arms. Most people would never have known that anyone was in the room, much less have been able to tell how that person had changed position. But Word Paynn wasn't most people. He had the uncanny ability to sense the things that others missed.

"Am I boring you, Moordryd?" Word asked, with a hint of irritation in his voice.

Surprised, the figure at the far end of the room straightened up and dropped his arms. Moordryd cursed himself for being caught with his guard down. He knew better than to think that he could fool Word Paynn.

But Moordryd couldn't help himself. The last thing he wanted was another history lesson. He already knew, that long ago, humans had bred the once pure and balanced gold-draconium dragons into new colors and energies. He was well aware that a major war, the Dragon-Human War, had erupted thousands of years ago and threatened life on the planet. Moordryd knew all of those things and much, much more. But deep down, he also knew that he didn't have any choice but to listen. After all, Word Paynn was his father.

"Three thousand years ago, the great

Dragon-Human War threatened to rip apart the planet," Word said. He looked at the screen in front of him with great interest. "But a single golden dragon, the last of its kind, chose a human to be his hero. He was called the Dragon Booster."

The screens glowed with the same image: a black-and-gold dragon with an armored rider perched on a tower of light. The light reached down and struck the other dragons, turning them gold.

"Together this Dragon Booster and the last gold dragon released the full power of the dragon," Word said. "They stopped the fight by turning all dragons back into their pure gold form."

Moordryd stepped toward the monitors for a closer look. He tried to avoid making eye contact with his father. Word's cold and determined stare never failed to send a chill down Moordryd's spine.

"I have learned, Moordryd, that the ancient gold-boned dragon has been bred back into existence," Word said, his calm voice hiding his excitement. "And by none other than my dear old friend, Connor Penn."

Word chuckled to himself. At one time, he and Connor Penn had been the best of friends. They were both orphans and had been raised by a secret order of Dragon Priests who had taught them about the ancient dragon world and the war.

As Word got older, he began to observe

the world and came to understand the dragons. He felt dragons were abused and that they should rule. He was expelled from the order for experimenting with dragon-control gear. The priests didn't understand him! Why couldn't they see the power the dragons were capable of releasing while wearing his gear? He and Connor had a huge fight. Connor thought that the gold dragon the priests talked about needed to return, and wanted to try to breed the powerful dragon. He did not agree with Word's plan to produce dragon-control gear. The two childhood friends ended up the farthest thing from best friends.

"Connor Penn is holding secret auditions for riders at Penn Stables," Word said. "And that's where you come in, Moordryd."

Moordryd looked up for the first time. The chance to figure in his father's plan pleased him. Moordryd craved his father's attention and, more important, his approval. But he made sure to hide those feelings behind a stony scowl.

"You will disguise yourself as an Elite Class racer, Moordryd," Word explained. His attention remained on the computer screens. "You will infiltrate Connor's racing stable and take the gold dragon."

Moordryd jumped on his father's words.

"Are you telling me how to steal a dragon, Father?" he sneered. "My Down City crew and I have been stealing them for you most of my life."

Word Paynn whipped around to face his son. His flowing robes billowed out behind him. Word obviously did not appreciate Moordryd's tone.

"This dragon must not choose a Dragon Booster!" Word declared. His gray eyes cut into Moordryd. "I will start a new dragon-human war. The gold dragon is the only thing that can stop me. And we can't allow that to happen. For when this war is over, I intend to rule the world!"

Moordryd liked the sound of what his father said. And then he thought the words he'd never dare say out loud: *Until it's my turn.*

CHAPTER 2

One mile below the place where Word and Moordryd Paynn stood in Sun City was Mid City, the second of Dragon City's seven levels. Mid City was only about three hundred years old. It was a strange combination of ancient architecture and modern buildings. Most of Dragon City's residents lived there, making it a cramped and noisy place.

Racetracks like those in Sun City snaked along throughout the three-mile expanse of Mid City. Mid City was home to the All-City racing circuit, the place where dragon racers aspired to Elite Class status. And at the center of the All-City racing circuit was Penn Stables. Penn Stables was the largest and most prestigious dragon stable in all of Dragon City. It was run by Connor Penn, a former champion dragon racer.

The entire Penn Stables complex appeared to hover in the air in the heart of Mid City. Its oval racetrack was an enormous ribbon of shimmering blue steel that encircled the compound. The inner circle of the track contained the compound's many dragon stalls, as well as the offices and residence of Connor Penn and his family.

A boy about sixteen years old stood with his back against one of the buildings. The teenager's name was Artha Penn. And nothing seemed to break his concentration. Not his chores—which included cleaning out the entire stables—and certainly not the dragons that passed by him from time to time. Artha's full attention was on something in his hand: a vid game controller.

From somewhere inside the stables, a dragon roared. But Artha didn't notice. The vid game was getting intense, and he didn't want to let anything make him lose his focus. Artha stared at the projected image suspended in the air before him. His hands expertly manipulated the vid controller's joysticks. Artha was starting to feel it. He was completely "in the zone."

Suddenly, a familiar face popped up on Artha's screen. It was Parmon Sean, Artha's best friend.

"Nice move, Artha!" Parmon said. "Now you're only three dragons behind me! Next time, use blue-draconium speed gear and red maneuvering gear on a white dragon and—"

"Everything's not all strategy, gear, and draconium energy, Parmon," Artha said.

Parmon was talking to Artha from his home on the other side of Mid City. Parmon was also a whiz at vid games. Together, he and Artha were designing what they hoped would become the biggest vid game around.

"Sometimes, Parm, it's just about being

really, really good!" Artha bragged.

Parmon watched the vid screen as Artha's dragon burst ahead of his own. "Drac, Artha! Do you have any idea what a great dragon racer you could be?" he said.

In addition to being Artha's best friend, Parmon was Artha's biggest fan. Parmon was always trying to convince Artha to take advantage of his natural ability to race dragons.

Artha rolled his eyes. "Real dragons? Ugh!" he moaned. "Let's just stick to perfecting our vid game, Parm. That's our ticket to fame and fortune."

A thunderous crash drew Artha's attention away from the game.

Across the way from him, two dragon racers were jostling dangerously around the main racetrack. Artha watched the dragons speed along the track. He noticed the racers employing different colors of gear to gain an advantage. Absorbed in the race, Artha didn't at first hear Parmon talking to him.

"Artha, I said is your dad still bugging you about racing and going to the academy?" asked Parmon.

"All the time," Artha sighed, looking back at his view screen. "It's like, everywhere I go, his dragons are following me."

As Artha spoke, he didn't notice the twelve-ton, black-and-gold dragon looming behind him. The dragon lowered his head and gave Artha a curious look. Artha glanced over at the dragon and shook his head.

"See what I mean, Parm?" Artha asked with a hint of exasperation. "Beau, I'm busy!"

Artha walked away from the dragon, and Parmon took advantage of the lull in conversation to move on to a different topic, one that really got him going.

"How do you like the new wireless controllers I built?" he asked eagerly. He motioned toward the device they were using to play the game. Before Artha had a chance to answer, Parmon went on to explain.

"I got hold of some draconium capacitors and rewired the bypass on the old gear contacts," he explained. "And then I rerouted the switching interfaces. . . ."

Artha, knowing that Parmon could go on like that for minutes at a time, fiddled with his vid game controller. A piece of his gear sparked and flew off. Parmon witnessed the whole thing on his view screen.

"It, uh, needs some tweaking. . . ." Parmon admitted.

Another piece of the controller sparked and jumped out of Artha's hand.

"Parm, the whole thing needs fixing!" Artha exclaimed.

Just then, the black-and-gold dragon caught up to Artha and peered over his shoulder. The boy struggled to push the dragon's enormous head aside, but the dragon wouldn't budge.

"Beau! Stop it!" Artha said to the

dragon. Beau's habit of popping up and nosing around was beginning to annoy him.

Beau gave Artha a playful nudge. The boy lost his balance and landed on the ground. His vid controller flew out of his hands and landed on the ground next to him. Artha might not have realized it, but pure gold dragons, like Beau, were just as smart as humans and perhaps even smarter. Beau knew exactly what he was doing.

"You know, you're like a big shadow!" Artha said. Frustrated, he finally figured out a surefire way to get the dragon out of his hair. Reaching inside his jacket, Artha grabbed an already-opened Draconee-Yum candy bar.

Beau bent down and grabbed the candy with his tongue. In one gulp, the bar was gone.

Artha knew that, like all dragons, who burn up tons of energy running at 200 miles per hour, Beau loved sweets.

"And if you keep eating candy like that, you'll be a big, *fat* shadow!" Artha teased.

Beau gave Artha's head a sloppy lick and turned away. It was at that moment that Artha noticed his vid controller lying directly in the dragon's path. But there was nothing he could do. Beau's foot crushed the vid gear flat.

"You see? This is exactly why I like video-game dragons better than real ones!" Artha grumbled. "Dumb dragon!"

Beau grunted and trotted off.

As Artha stood up, a boy bumped into him and knocked him back down again.

"Out of my way, stable boy!" the kid said.

The *kid* was none other than Moordryd Paynn. And he had no time to stop and chat with the help. He was on a mission.

CHAPTER 3

Artha couldn't believe the attitude of the boy who had pushed him.

Who is he to call me a stable boy? Artha wondered. He's the same age I am! Plus, my father owns and runs this place!

In an instant, Artha was back on his feet.

"'Stable boy'?" Artha said to the arrogant boy. "I'm Artha Penn. Of *Penn* Stables." He pointed to the gigantic Penn Stables sign that stood on top of the main building. The sign featured a giant portrait of Connor Penn. "Who are *you*?" asked Artha.

"I'm Moordryd Paynn, and I race dragons," the boy sneered. Then he noticed the shovel and long-handled scoop leaning against the wall behind Artha. "It looks like you clean up after them."

Moordryd chuckled at his own joke and took a step. *Squish!* He and Artha looked down at the same time and saw what Moordryd had stepped in.

Artha smiled. "Looks like you could use a little cleanup yourself," he smirked.

Moordryd seethed with anger, but then noticed Beau lurking in the distance. He took a deep breath.

"You're not worth the trouble,"

Moordryd muttered through clenched teeth, and he continued on his way. A young boy came up behind Artha.

"Who was that?" asked the boy.

"Nobody, Lance," Artha replied. He turned and looked at his little brother. Lance Penn had his father's red hair and a mischievous smile. He was also endlessly curious. But today his job was to help Artha clean up around the track.

"You missed a spot," Artha said. He pointed to the pile that Moordryd had stepped in.

"Why do I always get stuck cleaning up after the dragons?" Lance whined.

"Because you're my little brother, and you love helping

me," Artha replied, with a smile.

"I do?" Lance said. Then he looked up at Artha. "Wait a minute. No, I don't."

Artha playfully grabbed Lance and was about to throw him in a headlock when a shadow fell across the ground. Artha and Lance looked up.

"Dad!" Artha said. "Uh, I was just . . . you know . . ."

Connor Penn regarded Artha with a raised eyebrow.

"Yeah, I know," Artha said, releasing Lance. "Responsibilities . . ."

Connor smiled. He loved his sons and had always tried very hard to give them the kind of childhood he had missed out on. And while it wasn't easy being a single parent, Connor made every effort to keep things as normal as possible for the boys.

"Right, Artha," Connor said, trying to sound stern. "Around here, we—"

"—Help each other out," Artha nodded. "I know, Dad."

Lance grinned at Artha and handed him the shovel and scoop. Artha sighed but twirled the scoop like a ninja pooper-scooper pro. While Artha showed off his ninja skills, Connor looked over at the track. Beau stood there, looking as powerful as ever.

"Look at Beau," Connor said. "He's sixteen, just like you, Artha, ready to race and find out just what great things he's capable of."

Artha smiled. "Real subtle, Dad," he said. "Me . . . the dragon . . . great things on the horizon for us . . . I get it. Only I'm the one with the track shovel."

"I don't see you using it," Lance said teasingly. He really enjoyed moments like those, when he could play the little-brother card and get away with it.

"There are great things in store for all of you," Connor said warmly. "I should know. I raised you all from pups." He ruffled Lance's hair and walked toward the stables.

"And I helped raise you from a dork!" Artha said to Lance. He poked Lance in the rear with the shovel, then dropped it and ran.

"Hey, you!" Lance called. "Come back here!"

Word Paynn wants to start another dragon-human war. He needs to find the Black-and-Gold Dragon of Legend.

Moordryd Paynn listens as his father orders him to find the Dragon of Legend and capture him.

Artha Penn would rather race dragons on his vid
game than on a real track.

Parmon Sean, Artha's best friend, is a whiz at
science and at making gadgets. He made
Artha's vid game.

Beau—the newest racing dragon at Penn
Stables and the powerful Black-and-Gold
Dragon of Legend

Connor defends Beau when Moordryd sneaks into the stables.

Beau holds more power than anyone thought. Using a burst of magnetic energy, he breaks free from Moordryd's trap.

Penn Stables is under attack! Artha and Lance
race away from Moordryd's evil crew.

Artha now realizes he is the one meant to ride
Beau. He needs to get his brother to safety fast.

Beau has chosen Artha as his Dragon Booster!
The Dragon of Legend has returned to save
the world.

Artha holds the star mark his father gave him. It is now up to him to stop another dragon-human war. He is the Dragon Booster!

Lance chased Artha over to the track. As they turned the corner, Artha stopped short. Lance plowed right into him.

"What's the big idea?" Lance cried.

"Shhh!" Artha said, pointing.

Their father had gathered many Elite Class racers at the stable. He hoped one of those riders would be the one Beau would allow to ride him. Only Beau could choose the rider.

Lance popped out from behind Artha and saw a row of Elite Class dragon racers lined up. They stood along the outer edge of the Penn Stables racetrack facing the dragon stalls, and Connor stood facing them. He seemed to be speaking to one racer in particular. Artha and Lance crept closer so they could hear.

"I know you," Connor said. "You're Word Paynn's son."

Artha recognized him as the boy he'd met outside the dragon stalls.

"What are you going to do about it, old man?" Moordryd replied rudely.

Connor surveyed the angry young man and spied a crest that was partially hidden beneath Moordryd's jacket. He turned his gaze back to meet Moordryd's icy stare. Connor opened Moordryd's jacket and revealed the symbol.

"The mark of the Dragon Eye crew, huh?" Connor said. He stepped forward so the Moordryd had to look up at his face.

"Watch this!" Artha whispered to Lance from his hiding spot. "I'll bet Dad's going to let him have it!"

"My stables are off-limits to Down City crew members," Connor said. There was no trace of anger or irritation in his voice. Connor knew that, unlike the Elite Class racers, Down City crews were reckless with their powers and their dragons. "Go home, Moordryd. And tell your father that his old friend says . . . hello."

Moordryd glared up at Connor. Realizing that there wasn't anything he could do, he turned away with a snarl. On his way out, he passed Artha and Lance.

"Tell your father this isn't over," Moordryd warned.

CHAPTER 4

Watching Moordryd storm away, Connor's thoughts quickly flashed to his childhood, when he and Moordryd's father had been close friends.

They were both orphans and had been taken in by a secret order of Dragon Priests. They each received the same education, the same attention, the same guidance. Connor wondered, even to that day, how he and Word Paynn had ended up so different from each other.

Connor reached into his shirt and took out a star-shaped amulet. The golden medallion glistened in the sunlight. He squeezed it in his hand until the points pressed sharply into his flesh. Connor stuffed the amulet back inside his shirt and turned around once again to look at the racers.

"Thank you all for coming today," he said. "You are the best Street and Elite Class racers in Dragon City. And I want you all to meet my new dragon, Beau."

An enormous metal gate behind Connor began to open. On the other side of it stood Beau. His golden legs and tail were plainly visible. But the rest of his gold, black, and gray body was hidden beneath a layer of multicolored racing gear. Beau held his head high.

"Wow! What is that, Connor?" asked a racer in a green racing suit. "He's got level six white aero gear, five blue balance . . . and five red speed thruster!"

Connor nodded. "Beau can fully magnetize and use all gear types and levels," he said.

"A dragon that uses *all* gear colors?" one of the purple racers cried. "No dragon does that!"

Connor smiled slyly. "See for yourself," he said.

Beau narrowed his eyes and focused his draconium energy. With a blast, he let forth a burst of glowing magnetic power that grabbed a piece of green gear and a piece of red gear from two of the racers.

The gear whizzed through the air and slapped itself onto Beau's side.

There was silence in the stable as everyone stood watching in awe. Connor enjoyed the moment, in which the dragon racers grappled with what they saw. Dragons were supposed to be able to use only one color of gear. Beau's abilities were unheard of—at least by these racers. "So, who's going to be first?" Connor asked.

A blue Elite Class racer stepped forward. "It would be an honor," he said.

The racer carried

his helmet beneath his right arm. He walked slowly over to Beau. A stable hand rolled a ladder up beside the dragon while the racer put on his helmet. He took a deep breath and climbed the ladder. At the top, he threw his right leg over Beau's back and sat down.

No sooner had the ladder been pulled away than Beau generated a mag-burst that propelled the racer off Beau's back and sent him flying into the air. He almost reached the top of Connor's head in the picture on the giant Penn Stables sign. The racer landed with a dull splat in a mud pile next to the spot where Artha had started sweeping.

Connor was a little surprised by what Beau had done, but didn't let it show.

"Anyone else?" he asked.

None of the racers wanted to appear scared. A group of them surged forward to try their luck.

"One at a time," Connor said. "One at a time."

The next racer approached Beau and established eye contact, as if to signal that he, not Beau, was in charge. That racer barely had a chance to sit down on Beau's back before he, too, went flying through the air.

"WHOOOOOOAAAAA!" he cried, plowing directly into the Penn Stables sign before falling to the ground.

One after another, the racers tried their luck, but Beau kept throwing them. Artha and Lance looked on in amazement.

"Beau mags all gear . . ." Artha began.

". . . But not the riders," joked Lance.

"This is ridiculous," said a racer in a green suit. "Watch this!"

The racer took a running start, but before he could even leap onto Beau's back, the dragon roared and bit down on the racer's helmet. With a smug look, Beau spat it out. As he felt his head, the racer discovered that Beau had given him a brand-new bald spot!

After that, the handful of racers remaining were reluctant to volunteer. While they weren't necessarily afraid of Beau, they didn't relish the idea of flying through the air.

"It looks like Beau won't choose anybody today," Connor said. There was a trace of disappointment in his voice.

A sudden cloud of dust filled the stable. The ground trembled beneath the weight of an approaching dragon. The dragon screeched to a halt right in front of the other riders.

"Today's not over yet!" a girl shouted from the top of a red dragon.

The other racers looked over.

"Oh, great, it's Kitt Wonn," one of them whispered.

Kitt was a sixteen-year-old street-racing sensation. She seemed destined to be Dragon City's next dragon-racing champion. Needless to say, she wasn't very popular with the other racers. They were all jealous of her.

"There's not enough room on this track for her, her ego, and the rest of us," added another racer.

Kitt walked past the racers confidently. She knew the other racers were just jealous of her racing record. "You can all go home now," she said.

"What makes you think you can ride Beau and we can't?" a blue racer asked.

She stopped and turned around. "Well, let's see," Kitt said. "I beat you, and you, and you, and you." She pointed at each racer in the line. When she came to the last, she added, "And didn't I beat you last week in the Fire Cave? I thought so. Now, watch, and learn."

Kitt approached Beau with enormous confidence in her step. She walked all the way around the dragon before climbing the ladder. As she sat down on Beau's back, she looked over at Artha and smiled.

"She's on!" one of the racers shouted.

"And that's how it's done," Kitt said, folding her arms in triumph.

The racers cheered. But only Artha seemed to notice what looked like a tiny smile creeping across Beau's face.

CHAPTER 5

Kitt didn't stay on top of Beau for long. Beau winked at Artha, and in an instant, Artha seemed to understand what he had in mind. With a fierce mag-burst, Beau launched Kitt higher into the air than he had any of the other racers. Fortunately, when she came down, she missed the mud pile. Unfortunately, she landed right on top of Artha.

As they lay there nose to nose, Artha smiled. "Right . . . so, uh, *that's* how it's done," he said to Kitt.

"*Arrrrggghhhh!*" Kitt grunted, pushing herself up and far away from Artha. She got to her feet and dusted off her racing suit.

Artha stood up, laughing, and he thought he saw Beau laugh as well. When he looked again, Beau just stood there.

"Anybody else?" Connor called out with the trace of a smile on his lips. He looked around at the Elite Class racers. These were the best racers in Dragon City. He hoped at least one more would have the courage to step forward.

But none of the remaining racers wanted to try any longer. They all shook their heads. They had seen too many riders flung from the back of the mighty Beau and thrown to the ground.

"Well, I guess that's it, then. . . ." Connor shrugged.

"Wait," Kitt said. She moved over and stood next to Connor. "What about your son?" She motioned to Artha. "What about the stable boy?"

"Yeah, what about the *stable boy*?" echoed Lance. He looked up at his brother and grinned.

Artha glared at his little brother. Then a feeling of anger started to boil up inside him.

"You know, this stable boy thing is really beginning to scrape my scales," he said.

Connor nodded and made his way to Artha's side. The older Penn took off his racing jacket and draped it over Artha's shoulders.

"Here, you can wear my old racing jacket," he said. "You *do* race really well in your dragon vid game."

Artha tried to shrug the jacket off. "Exactly," he said. "It's just a game!" Artha didn't want any part of this live-action racing.

Connor put a reassuring hand on his son's shoulder.

"Artha, listen. This isn't that different from your vid games. And plus, it's Beau— he's followed you around his whole life." Connor paused, and his voice grew more serious. "The dragon is just like the great power within you. Relax, open your mind and your heart, and release that power.

Release the dragon."

Out of the corner of his eye, Artha saw Kitt, with a smug little smile on her face. She was tapping her foot impatiently.

"Come on, stable boy," she taunted. "Let's see what you've got!" Always up for a challenge, Kitt was showing off her highly competitive side.

Even Beau looked at Artha. He cocked his head and regarded his new challenger.

Artha could feel everyone staring at him. He really didn't want to get up on the very large dragon in front of all those people, but he knew he'd never live it down if he didn't try. He took a deep breath. He could do this. He knew how to ride a dragon. . . . Right? Just hop on, he thought.

"Okay, okay," he said. "Let's do it."

He zipped up his father's jacket and grabbed a helmet that Lance found for him. Then he cautiously walked up to Beau.

"Okay, boy," he said, stroking Beau's neck. "You, uh, didn't catch that 'dumb dragon' thing before, right? You know I was only kidding."

Artha grabbed the rails of the stepladder and slowly climbed up. He'd climbed that ladder a hundred times before when he was cleaning up around the stables. But he'd never climbed up to get onto a dragon. That was probably why those ten little steps going up felt more like ten miles.

Artha looked down at Kitt, who was smiling at him. For some reason, her attitude gave Artha a tiny bit of courage. Artha smiled back.

Just then, Beau noticed something sticking out of Lance's pocket. It was a Draconee-Yum bar. He reached down for the chocolate with his big dragon head. With his tongue he snatched the candy bar from Lance's pocket.

The sudden shift in position caught Artha off guard, and he lost his balance. With a yelp, he tumbled off the ladder and landed on the track with a thud.

Kitt and the other racers burst out laughing. Artha jumped up, threw down the jacket, and stormed away. "You see? This is exactly why I don't like real dragons!" he shouted over his shoulder. He wanted nothing more than to get as far from Beau as possible.

Connor shot the racers a cold look. They instantly stopped laughing.

"That's all for today," Connor said. He wanted to go after Artha.

The racers dispersed while Connor went to find Artha. It wasn't until much later that he finally caught up to him. He found him outside Beau's stable, eating a candy bar.

"Well, that was totally embarrassing," Artha said when he looked up and saw his father standing there. "Let's do it again sometime!"

Connor was not a big fan of Artha's sarcasm, but considering the circumstances, he simply smiled. He knew his son.

"When you're ready," Connor said.

"What if I'm never ready?" asked Artha.

"Believe in yourself, Artha, and others will believe in you." Once again, Connor put his hand on Artha's shoulder. "Come on, son, tomorrow's another day. Maybe Beau will choose a rider then."

Beau suddenly shot his tongue out through a small opening in the stable wall and grabbed Artha's candy bar.

"The only thing this dragon ever seems to choose is my candy bars!" Artha exclaimed.

Connor laughed. As they walked away, neither of them noticed a shadowy figure watching them in the distance.

CHAPTER 6

Beau finished the candy bar in the blink of an eye. He was particularly fond of sweets. In fact, most dragons were. Their bodies turned the sugar into the massive amounts of energy they needed in order to magnetize gear to their bodies and in order to race. But tonight the only reason Beau needed the candy bar was that he hadn't had dessert.

Now that it was early evening, Beau lazed around his stall waiting for Connor

Penn to make his final rounds. Beau was in the middle of a stretch when he heard a sound outside. But instead of the usual soft *click* of the lock opening, he heard another sound. It was more of a *zap*, followed by a heavy thud. Beau sensed that something wasn't right.

His stall door flew open. The person standing in the doorway wasn't Connor Penn. That much Beau knew. The figure stepped out of the shadows. If he had known what to look for, Beau would have noticed the Dragon Eye crew symbol on the stranger's jacket. Or he might have seen the mirrored face mask and put himself on guard.

Before Beau could react, the stranger pulled a telescoping turquoise flash stick from his coat. He jammed one end into the ground in front of Beau. A blinding flash filled the stall and stunned the young dragon.

The stranger moved quickly. He fired several bursts of light, to disorient Beau.

Beau narrowed his eyes and tensed his enormous body. The golden lines along Beau's muscular frame throbbed with energy. He generated a fierce blast of magnetic power that sent the stranger sailing out of the stable.

"Using your mag-burst to repel the draconium in my suit?" the stranger said as he got up. "Let's see what you do with this!"

The stranger approached with a short purple canister. He flicked his wrist and the canister extended itself into a long purple staff. He prepared to attack. Just then, light again flooded the stall, but this time from outside. The stranger turned to see Connor Penn standing in the doorway.

"Get away from my dragon!" Connor yelled.

"Stay out of this, old man," the intruder replied. He lunged out of the stall—right for Connor.

Connor jumped up and somersaulted through the air over the stranger's head.

The stranger responded swiftly. He spun around and leaped back at Connor.

The two of them began an acrobatic exchange of jumps, kicks, and flips in the middle of Beau's stall.

Connor parried with his blue staff. "Not bad . . ." he said, noticing the boy's fine

skills. "But you're too angry . . . too reckless. . . ."

In one move, Connor threw the stranger against the stable wall, knocking off the mirrored mask.

"Moordryd Paynn?" Connor said as the

mask hit the floor. He sighed. Connor should have known that Word Paynn would have stooped to that kind of behavior.

"This isn't over, old man!" Moordryd warned as he stood up. "You don't know what you just started. You'll see!"

Moordryd raced out of the stable and disappeared into the shadows.

Connor immediately turned his attention to Beau. He removed the rest of the harness and deactivated the black electrical prods. Some of the gear remained dangling from the dragon's side.

"You okay, Beau?" he asked. He stroked the mighty dragon's neck.

Beau gave Connor a slight nudge on the cheek.

"Ah, Word, my old friend," Connor continued. "You will stop at nothing to get this dragon." Concern grew within Connor. Considering the events of the day, he realized that the situation was growing serious. Word Paynn's limitless resources made it inevitable that he would eventually succeed.

Connor looked at Beau. He knew that this dragon was his only hope. "Time is running out," he said, to no one in particular. "Beau must choose. And soon."

"Dad! Dad!" Artha called, running into the stable. "I heard noises! What's going on?"

Artha found his father looking tired and Beau breathing heavily, as if he had just run a hard race.

"I saw the lock on the ground outside the door," Artha said. "It looks like someone used light-green deactivation gear to break the lock. Is everything okay?"

Connor reached inside his shirt and grabbed a chain from around his neck. He held the chain out.

"Come here, Artha," he said. "It's time I told you the truth."

Puzzled, Artha stepped forward.

"Dad, is this another one of your racing medals?" he asked. "Because, while I really like them, I already have, like, a hundred of them and—"

"Artha, I've had this since I was sixteen," Connor said. "Just as you are now." Connor placed the chain around Artha's neck.

Artha felt something dangling against his chest. He looked down and saw a strange, star-shaped amulet hanging at the end of the chain. He carefully lifted it up for a closer look.

"I've never seen anything like this before," Artha said. "Dad, what is this thing?"

As Artha examined the star amulet on the chain, he realized that his dad was giving him something important. But he had no idea why.

CHAPTER 7

"This amulet was given to me by a secret order of Dragon Priests," Connor explained to Artha. "The ones who raised me as their son. They told me of an ancient legend."

Artha looked at the round disk in his father's hand. "Legend?" he asked. "What kind of legend?"

Connor saw that the moment had come when he must tell his son the truth about the past.

"Artha, when I was a young boy, not quite Lance's age, I lost my parents," he began quietly. "I was taken in by the Dragon Priests. They raised me in the ways of dragon lore and taught me to respect dragons."

Artha nodded as the information sank in. "I guess that explains this place, then," he said.

Connor didn't seem to notice Artha's attempt at humor. He continued with his story.

"The Dragon Priests spoke of a coming war between dragons and humans," he said. "This war can only be stopped by the return of the Black-and-Gold Dragon of Legend. And only when the special dragon chooses a true human hero who can release his secret powers. That human is called the Dragon Booster."

What was his father talking about? Artha wondered. And what did all of it have to do with this weird necklace and amulet?

"Dragon Booster?" Artha asked. "What does that mean? And why are you giving this to me?"

"I want you to keep it safe in case anything happens," Connor said. "If Beau truly is the Dragon of Legend, and if he chooses a rider, the very same star mark that is on that amulet will emerge on Beau's head. If that happens— *when* that happens— give this amulet to the chosen one. The one Beau chooses will be the Dragon Booster."

Artha looked into his father's eyes. He felt there was something else his father wanted to tell him. But before Artha could ask, his father smiled.

"Now let's give Beau a chance to get some sleep," he said. "And you, too, for that matter. Go on back to the house, and I'll see you later. I want to make sure everything else is secure around here. "

Connor disappeared into the stable.

As Artha walked back to the residence, he found that he was having a hard time wrapping his brain around everything his father had told him. He tucked the amulet into his shirt. When he got home, he decided to try to take his mind off everything that had just happened.

He found Lance in the kitchen playing a vid game and wondered what had happened to his own vid-game gear. On the table he spotted the crushed vid game controller. He tried to salvage what was left of it. Sitting with Lance in the kitchen, Artha didn't notice the group of dark figures creeping through the shadows beneath the window.

"It's no use," Artha sighed. "Parm's going to have to completely rebuild this one."

Lance looked up. "Better tell him that he'd better make it dragon-proof," he joked. Artha smiled and tossed the pieces of the controller back onto the table. Then he heard a sound from outside. He looked out the window, and something caught his eye. In the darkness, he thought he saw somebody run by with a Dragon Eye crest on his jacket.

"Stay here, Lance," Artha said.

He quietly slipped outside and began to follow another shadowy figure with the same Dragon Eye crest on his jacket. Just as he rounded the corner of one of the stables, a loud explosion shook the night. Artha turned and saw part of the residence burst into flames.

"Dad! Lance!" he cried as he raced toward the building. "Hang on, I'm on my way!"

The Dragon Eye crew continued on its mission to capture Beau. They burst into the dragon's stall. Moordryd Paynn, the leader of the Dragon Eye crew, was ready to carry out the plan and took command.

"Green trapping gear . . . now!" he ordered.

One of the crew members threw a green trapping module that stuck to Beau's chest. Glowing green cables shot out of the module and stuck to the walls, preventing Beau from surging forward.

"Black control gear!" Moordryd commanded.

The crew members slapped several circular black disks onto Beau's upper leg. Black metal extensions shot out and began forcing the dragon to his knees by using his own energy against him.

Beau gathered his strength and surged

with even more magnetic energy.

"Mag-burst!" warned Cain, Moordryd's right-hand man in situations like these.

A shock wave of magnetic energy blasted off Beau's back. Three of the crew members flew across the stall and slammed into the wall. When it was all over, Beau lay on the ground, exhausted. He had used up all of his energy and was now at the mercy of his captors. Moordryd stood over him and smiled triumphantly.

Artha reached the house; it was being consumed by flames. He bravely ran inside.

"Lance?" he shouted. "Dad?"

Artha noticed Lance poke up his head from behind the kitchen table. It had been blown on its side by the blast and was protecting Lance from the falling debris.

"Are you okay, Lance?" Artha asked.

Lance nodded.

"Where's Dad?" Artha continued.

"I couldn't find him," Lance replied.

A creaking sound warned Artha of something bad to come. He dived behind the table where Lance was just as part of the ceiling collapsed, blocking the doorway, their only way out.

"We're trapped!" Lance cried. "Help!"

CHAPTER 8

Artha's and Lance's cries for help floated across the compound.

Beau's sensitive ears picked up the sound, and something stirred deep inside him. Realizing that Artha and Lance were in trouble, Beau summoned his strength. With all his might, he slowly rose up. The black control gears on his legs broke apart and shot off in all directions.

Moordryd couldn't believe it. He knew this dragon was special, but never would he have thought that black control gear could be broken apart like that.

"Impossible! He's breaking free!" Moordryd cried. "Stop him! I want that dragon!"

The other crew members ran into Beau's stall from the outer stable. But Beau was ready.

"Hold on! Another mag-burst!" Moordryd warned his crew.

Beau powered up and fired off an immense mag-burst. The flash of energy knocked everyone in the stall against the walls. Beau tore through the green trapping gear and launched himself forward. He broke through the stable wall and charged right toward the residence.

Inside the burning house, Artha desperately searched for a way to get Lance out. Then he spotted something near the top of the wall.

"There! The air vent!" Artha instructed. "It leads outside."

He grabbed Lance and hoisted him up. Lance pulled the grating off and dropped back to the ground.

"But it's way too small for you, Artha!" Lance said.

"Go!" Artha said, pushing Lance back up and through the vent.

Lance squeezed through the opening and disappeared. Artha spun around, hoping to find some way out for himself. He couldn't imagine never seeing Lance or his father again. But he also couldn't imagine how he'd ever be able to escape. He pulled the amulet from around his neck and held it tightly in his hand.

But then the unimaginable happened.

Beau blasted through the wall, with a deafening crash. Artha dived for cover. When he looked up, he saw Beau standing over him.

"Beau! Am I glad to see you!" Artha cried. "Let's get out of here before this place falls on our heads!"

Artha jumped onto Beau's back. Instantly, Beau's head arched up and his body stiffened. The draconium deep within his bones began to glow, generating a fierce energy. His whole body began to shake.

"B—B—Beau?" said Artha.

An intense golden light began to radiate from Beau's body. And then, right before Artha's eyes, a Gold Star–Mark emerged near the top of Beau's head. The star mark fired a beam of golden light straight up to the heavens. A mighty hum filled the air, and Artha began to hear his father's voice deep inside his own head: *The one Beau chooses will be the Dragon Booster.*

Artha swallowed. "Me?"

With another blast of energy, Beau blew out the back wall of the house and took off, Artha on his back. They raced out into the compound and found Lance. Artha reached down and scooped his brother up onto Beau's back.

"You mean Beau chose *you*?" Lance asked. He had been stunned to see his brother sitting comfortably on the mighty dragon's back.

Artha just shrugged as Beau carried them into the shadows. There, he heard another voice, this time from across the compound.

He turned and saw Moordryd Paynn and his crew on their dragons.

"Everyone split up and find that dragon

immediately!" Moordryd yelled.

The crew members dispersed through-out the compound, leaving Moordryd and Cain. Moordryd was not about to give up.

"I know that dragon's around here somewhere, Cain," Moordryd said. "He may be strong, but he's no match for me and Decepshun." Moordryd gave his black dragon a slap on the neck. Decepshun grunted and scanned the compound, his own dragon sense guiding him.

Meanwhile, Beau stealthily dashed over to the edge of the retaining wall. The wall surrounded the entire compound and served as the outer boundary of the Penn Stables property. Just beyond it lay the rest of Mid City—a mile straight down.

Beau draped his tail over the retaining

wall. Artha and Lance slid down to the narrow ledge below. Then Beau slid away as quietly as he had arrived.

"What's going on?" Lance asked.

"You got me," Artha answered. "I guess all we can do now is sit tight. And whatever you do, don't look down." The thought of perching on that skinny ledge in the middle of the sky didn't exactly thrill Artha. But he knew he had to put on a good show, if only to keep Lance from freaking out. The thing was, Lance was far from freaking out. He lay down and leaned over the edge so that his head dangled in the air.

"Hey, look at me, Artha!"

Lance called. "I'm flying over Dragon City!"

Artha pulled Lance back from the edge.

"For once in your life, just sit still, okay?" Artha said. He wondered why Beau had left them there and what the dragon was up to.

Beau remained in the shadows of the Penn Stables compound, quietly studying Moordryd. A quick upward glance had told Beau everything he needed to know. The mighty Penn Stables sign atop the main building was unsteady.

Beau growled and sprang from the shadows.

"There!" Moordryd cried. "Get him!"

Moordryd and Cain advanced toward Beau. But before they could release any of their capture gear, the mighty dragon slammed his tail into the base of the building. The shock wave knocked loose the shaky Penn Stables sign, and the giant likeness of Connor Penn slammed to the ground, directly in front of Moordryd and Cain. Cain's dragon reared up, almost throwing Cain to the ground. Decepshun stood still as Moordryd watched Beau disappear over the ledge.

CHAPTER 9

When Beau appeared on the ledge where Artha and Lance stood, they were very relieved. They climbed back onto Beau's back, and, immediately, Artha felt better. But then he looked around and realized that Beau would never be able to climb all the way back over the wall again.

"This is ridiculous," Artha said. "We're stuck on this ledge overlooking all of Dragon City, and there's no way out!"

Lance surveyed their options.

"How about that building?" he said. "It looks like it has a nice flat roof." He pointed to a rooftop a full mile down.

Artha thought Lance was crazy. "No dragon can jump that far!" he said.

But Beau took one quick glance and sized things up. Then, taking an enormous dragon breath, he began racing along the length of the ledge. Beau knew that he could make that jump easily.

"Beau! What are you doing?" Artha exclaimed. "You can't jump! It's too far!" He squeezed his eyes shut and once again heard his father's voice deep inside his mind: *The dragon is just like the great power within you. Release that power. . . . Release the dragon!*

Artha felt the breeze against his face.

He took a deep breath and tried to relax.

Release the dragon, he repeated to himself.

Artha felt a wave of energy wash over him as Beau leaped off the ledge. The Gold Star–Mark on Beau's head burned brightly. The dragon soared through the sky over Mid City. Time itself seemed to slow to a crawl. And Artha felt a strange sensation. It felt as if he and Beau were somehow connected.

Artha opened his eyes as the roof beneath them rapidly approached. Panic took over, and he lost all interest in being relaxed. His immediate concern involved landing on the roof without breaking his neck.

Beau hit the roof in a shower of sparks

as his claws tried to slow down. The dragon skidded across the rooftop and slammed into a billboard at the far edge of the roof.

Artha and Lance didn't make the smoothest landing, either. They tumbled off Beau's back with a thump. "We made it?" Artha said, shaking his head. He looked around and saw that they were no longer in motion. "We made it!"

Lance stuck his head out of the garbage can in which he had landed. "Speak for yourself," he said.

Taking care to stay hidden, Artha glanced up and noticed Moordryd and Cain searching for them at the far end of the ledge.

"We'd better get out of here," Artha said. This was no time to get caught.

The brothers quickly took cover and disappeared behind the billboard.

A mile above them, Moordryd readied Decepshun to pursue Beau.

"He's getting away," Moordryd said. "Come on!"

Cain reached out and grabbed Moordryd's arm.

"Our dragons won't jump that far," he warned.

Moordryd shook off Cain's grip.

"Speak for yourself!" he retorted.

Moordryd rode Decepshun over the wall at the far end of the ledge; Decepshun began running along the ledge just as Beau had done.

Just before reaching the edge, Decepshun skidded to a stop. Moordryd glared down, furious both that his dragon had defied him and that he had let Beau escape. He instructed Cain to gather the crew and return to the Dragon Eye compound in Down City.

Carefully, Artha, Lance, and Beau followed Moordryd and his crew all the way down to Squire's End. Squire's End was more than seven miles below Artha and Lance's Mid City home at Penn Stables.

It was located in Down City, the most dangerous place in all of Dragon City. This part of Dragon City was mostly in shadows. The only light came from the flickering billboards that dotted the cityscape and the neon warnings and markings of the twelve Down City crews.

Artha and Lance managed to find a deserted alley. It was filled with junk and poorly lit, but at least it provided a place where they could hide with Beau. The first thing Artha did was to call Parmon. Parmon quickly arrived on his dragon, Cyrano.

"Artha, what are you doing in Squire's End?" asked Parmon. "This is Down City crew territory. Dragon City security doesn't even come down here."

"Somebody tried to steal Beau, and this is where he stopped running," Artha explained. He checked to make sure Lance was not within earshot. "Did you see my father? He's not answering my calls."

"I checked the stables," Parmon reported. "All I found was this."

Parmon held out Connor's racing jacket. It was partially burned.

"I saw the symbol of the crew that attacked the stable: a black dragon eye," Artha said. "They're the ones responsible for what happened."

Parmon looked around warily. He didn't like being there and wanted to convince Artha it was time to go.

"Look, Artha, the Down

City crews have spies all over," he began. "If they want your dragon, they can track you down. They can pay people to talk. They can—"

"I'm hungry!" Lance announced.

"And what about food?" Parmon continued. "Do you realize how much a dragon like Beau needs to eat? Why, just to maintain his base draconium levels, he'd—"

Artha searched his mind. His best friend was right. With Connor missing, a hungry dragon, an even hungrier little brother, and nothing but questions, Artha needed a plan, and fast. It hit him like a mag-burst.

"I'm going to street-race, Parm," Artha said.

For the first time in a long time, Parmon Sean was at a loss for words.

"Wh—wh—wh—what?" was all he could manage.

"The best defense is a good offense!" Artha declared. "We need money. We need to eat. And Down City crews race in the All-City races. They're after my dragon, and they attacked my father's stable. I'm going after them!"

Even though Parmon had never seen Artha so decisive, he was still uneasy about his friend's decision.

"But you can't!" he said. "They'll identify Beau and make another attempt to steal him. And don't think this time they'll let him get away."

Artha took a deep breath. He knew that

Parmon was right. He couldn't bear the thought of risking Beau's safety, especially after the way the dragon had saved him and Lance from the fire. Artha walked over and tapped Beau's neck gently.

"Then Beau will stay here . . . and I'll race another dragon," he said. "Sorry, boy."

Beau looked into Artha's eyes. In an instant, Beau summoned his energy and released a blinding flash of golden light. When Artha, Lance, and Parmon opened their eyes, they couldn't believe what they saw. Beau looked like a totally different dragon.

"Did you see that? He changed color!" Lance exclaimed. "That's totally drac!"

Beau stood before them, but now the

Black-and-Gold Dragon of Legend was red and blue.

"I see it; I just don't believe it!" Parmon said. "Artha, what does it mean?"

"It means you can race Beau!" Lance said, answering for his brother.

Artha smiled as he pulled out the star-shaped amulet.

"It means I can do a lot more than that!" he declared. "Just wait!"